Building the
SYDNEY
HARBOUR
BRIDGE

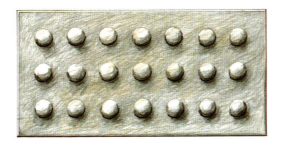

John Nicholson

ALLEN & UNWIN

Acknowledgements

I acknowledge and am grateful for information provided by the following sources:

J.J.C. Bradfield, *The Sydney Harbour Bridge and City Railway – Report of Engineer*
(H. Phillips, Willoughby NSW, 1903?)

F.Cash, *Parables of the Sydney Harbour Bridge* (F. Cash, Sydney, 1930)

H. Cazneaux, *The Bridge Book* (Ure Smith/Art in Australia, Sydney, 1930)

H. Cazneaux, *The Second Bridge Book* (Ure Smith/Art in Australia, Sydney, 1931)

R.E. Curtis, *The Bridge* (Currawong Press, Sydney, 1981)

H.E. Dance, *Sydney Harbour Bridge* (Nelson, London, 1946)

D. Ellyard and R. Raxworthy, *The Proud Arch, the Story of the Sydney Harbour Bridge*
(Bay Books, Sydney, 1982)

Institute of Engineers, Australia, *The Construction of the Sydney Harbour Bridge* (video)

H. Mallard, *Building the Sydney Harbour Bridge* (Sun Books/ACP, Melbourne, 1976)

H. Phillips, *Sydney Harbour Bridge* (H. Phillips, Willoughby NSW, 1931)

U. Prunster, *The Sydney Harbour Bridge 1932–82* (Angus & Robertson/AGNSW, Sydney,
1982)

The Pylon Museum

R. Raxworthy, From Footbridge to Harbour Bridge, the Life and Works of J.J.C. Bradfield
(Bridgeclimb, Sydney, 1999)

The Story of the Sydney Harbour Bridge (n.s., Sydney, 1970?)

P. Spearritt, *The Sydney Harbour Bridge – A Life* (George Allen & Unwin, Sydney, 1982)

Allen & Unwin
9 Atchison Street
St Leonards NSW 2065
Australia
Phone: (61 2) 8425 0100
Fax: (61 2) 9906 2218
Email: frontdesk@allen-unwin.com.au
Web: http://www.allen-unwin.com.au

National Library of Australia
Cataloguing-in-Publication entry:

Nicholson, John, 1950–.
     Building the Sydney Harbour Bridge.

     Bibliography.
     Includes Index.
     ISBN 1 86508 259 7.
     ISBN 1 86508 258 9 (pbk.).

     1. Sydney Harbour Bridge (Sydney, N.S.W.) – Design and construction –
Juvenile literature. 2. Bridges, Arched – New South Wales – Sydney –
Design and construction – Juvenile literature. I. Title.

624.67099441

Designed by John Nicholson and Sandra Nobes
Printed by South China Printing Co., Hong Kong

▼ Commuters at Milson's Point ferry terminal. In 1922, Sydneysiders made 40 million ferry trips from one side of the harbour to the other

A Tale of Two Cities

Sydney was once two cities. On the south shore lived 600 000 people, while across the harbour lived another 300 000. Dozens of ferries carried people to and fro, but most food and other goods went the long way, across the Gladesville Bridge – a trip that could take several hours. People had been talking for decades about building some sort of harbour crossing – a bridge, perhaps, or a tunnel. One rather lateral idea had been to cut a canal for ships between Lavender Bay and Neutral Bay, and then use the rock removed from the canal to build a causeway across the harbour. But it remained one of those problems that seemed just too difficult, too expensive, to solve – that is, until 1922.

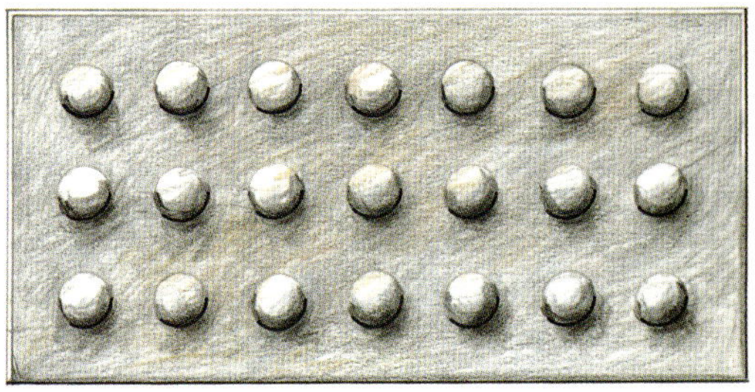

▼ **Sydney, 1922, shown in red**

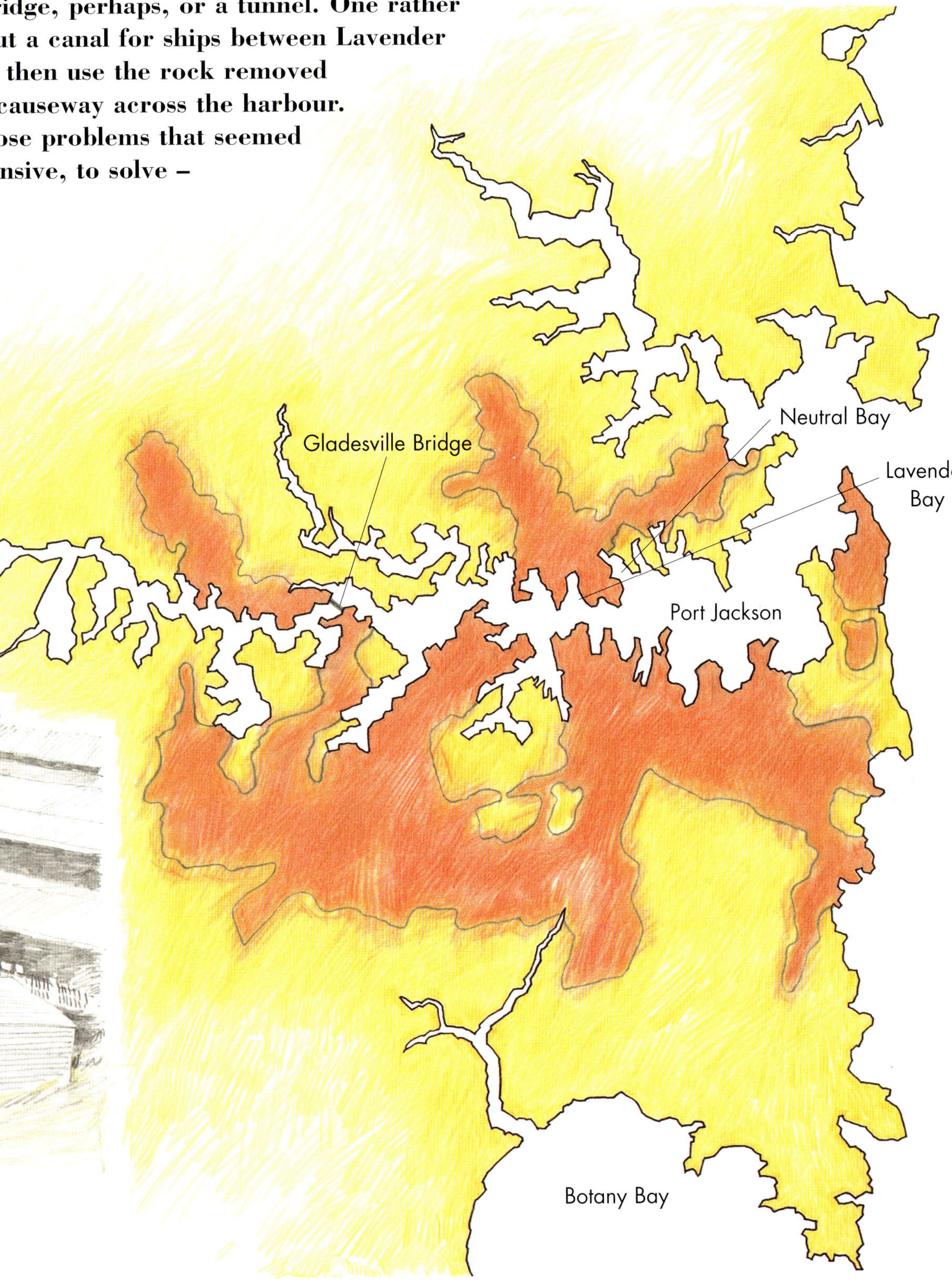

Neutral Bay

Gladesville Bridge

Lavender Bay

Port Jackson

Botany Bay

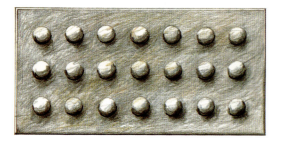

Bridging the Gap

In 1922 the New South Wales parliament finally got serious and passed the Sydney Harbour Bridge Act. Bridge-builders from all round the world were invited to submit designs and prices for a bridge to satisfy the broad requirements drawn up by government engineers.

---

16 January 1924

Tenders close on this day. Twenty proposals are received from six different companies.

24 March 1924

Contracts are signed by the government and the winning tenderer, Dorman, Long and Company.

▼ **A 1900 competition attracted this rather futuristic entry submitted by a syndicate called 'Wait and Hope'!**

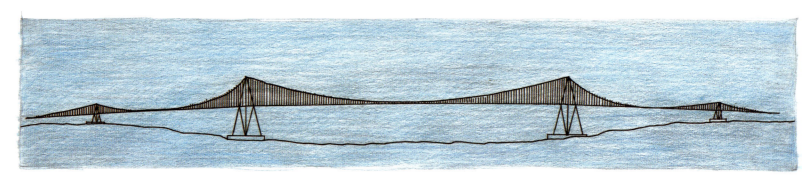

...and this more elaborately decorated design ▼

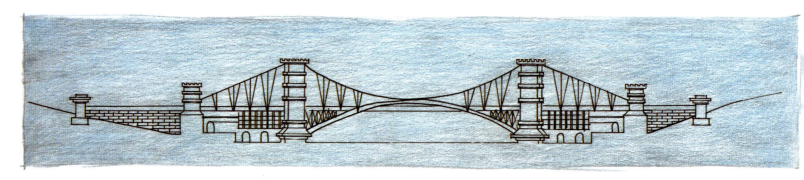

▼ **Dorman, Long and Company's successful 1924 design was this steel-arched bridge**

Dorman, Long's winning entry was a two-hinged, steel-arch bridge with five approach spans at each end; total length 1149 metres. It would cost the government £4 217 722 (worth about $250 million today).

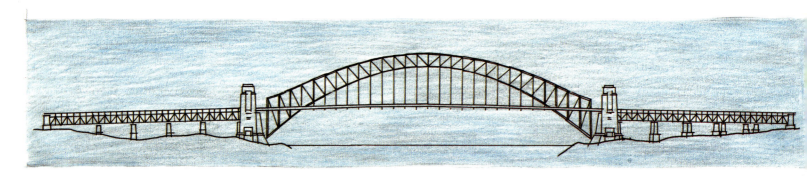

J.J.C.Bradfield

During construction of the bridge, Bradfield kept a close eye on the work. He was always there for difficult or important stages, but he would also pop up in unexpected places at unexpected moments. Bradfield and his team of inspectors demanded a very high standard of work, ordering 101 559 rivets to be cut out and replaced! Lots of other steelwork rejected by the inspectors was dumped in the harbour – one joker remarking that they didn't really need a bridge because you could walk all the way across the harbour on dumped steel.

Bradfield's friendly and sympathetic attitude towards the workers made him popular. He wasn't a particularly imposing figure in his trademark battered hat and scruffy clothes. On one occasion a supervisor, thinking that he was someone trying to get work on the bridge, refused to give him a job!

Bradfield was a man of immense talent and ability, a human dynamo who embraced life with enormous energy and enthusiasm.

One of ithe winning features of Dorman, Long's bid was that it was to be largely 'Australian-made'. As much of the steel as possible, and all of the stone, sand and cement, would be locally produced. All the individual pieces of the bridge would be put together in Australia, using Australian labour.

Steel-arch bridges were popular in the early twentieth century, eclipsing the earlier 'cantilever' type. Steel-arch designs later gave way to steel suspension bridges.

Who Built the Bridge?

The government engineer in charge of the project was John Job Crew Bradfield. He was really the 'father' of the Sydney Harbour Bridge. In 1912 the New South Wales government had appointed him 'Chief Engineer for Metropolitan Railway Construction and Sydney Harbour Bridge'. He had a grand plan for Sydney's transport, and the harbour bridge was its central feature. Now, after 10 years of preparation, planning and false starts (remember there was a world war on between 1914 and 1918), his dream was about to come true.

The construction company, Dorman, Long and Co., was an English steel manufacturer and bridge-builder. Their engineer-in-charge in Sydney was Laurence Ennis. He supervised the construction of the bridge. They employed another engineer, Sir Ralph Freeman, to design the bridge in detail, calculating the sizes of all the pieces of steel, and working out how to join them together. He had a large team of engineers and draftsmen to help him.

A Bitter Quarrel

In April 1928, when the bridge construction was well advanced, an argument broke out between Bradfield and Freeman, both claiming to have designed the bridge. Bradfield was probably right to claim responsibility for the overall look of the bridge, but Freeman appears to have come up with the same sort of idea at the same time. He was certainly responsible for the enormous amount of detailed designing involved. The two men argued bitterly about it, and their relationship remained strained to the end.

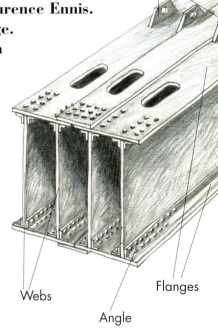

▲ **One length of the bottom chord**

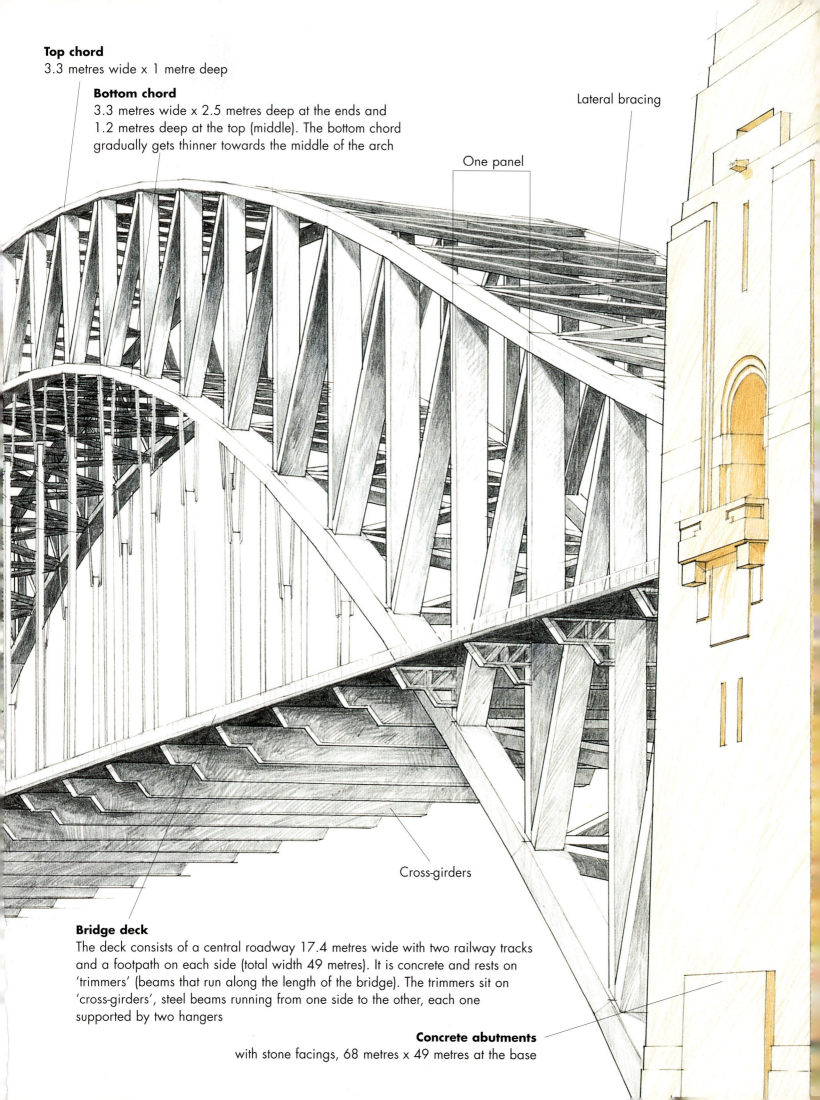

Top chord
3.3 metres wide x 1 metre deep

Bottom chord
3.3 metres wide x 2.5 metres deep at the ends and
1.2 metres deep at the top (middle). The bottom chord
gradually gets thinner towards the middle of the arch

Lateral bracing

One panel

Cross-girders

Bridge deck
The deck consists of a central roadway 17.4 metres wide with two railway tracks
and a footpath on each side (total width 49 metres). It is concrete and rests on
'trimmers' (beams that run along the length of the bridge). The trimmers sit on
'cross-girders', steel beams running from one side to the other, each one
supported by two hangers

Concrete abutments
with stone facings, 68 metres x 49 metres at the base

The Winning Design

Let's have a closer look at the sort of bridge that Dorman, Long had agreed to build for the New South Wales government.

The main span, across the water, is a steel arch. More accurately, it's actually two arches, side by side, about 30 metres apart. Each arch is a 'truss'. That means it's made up of a whole lot of 'sticks' of steel arranged in a series of triangles. Triangles are a very strong, stable arrangement – you can't force a triangle out of shape, as you can a square. The roadway or 'deck' is hung from the two arches.

At each end of the arch there's a concrete 'abutment' that stops the two ends of the arch from spreading outwards. On top of each abutment there are two high stone and concrete towers or 'pylons'. Bradfield had asked for the pylons to be added to the original design. They are there for decoration – they don't hold anything up.

Five pairs of smaller steel trusses at each end of the bridge – the 'approach spans' – are supported by concrete piers (thick posts). They extend the bridge over the low-lying land on either side of the harbour.

Facts and Figures

Length of arch: 503 metres
Total length of bridge: 1149 metres
Highest point: 134 metres above sea level
Weight of steel in arch: 37 000 tonnes
Total weight of steel: 52 800 tonnes
Time to build: 7 years and 356 days
Final cost: over £10 000 000
(worth about $750 000 000 today)

During 1926 Bradfield arranged to have six sheets of steel painted different colours. The six samples were left out in the weather before a final decision was made about the final colour of the bridge. It's still the same colour today.

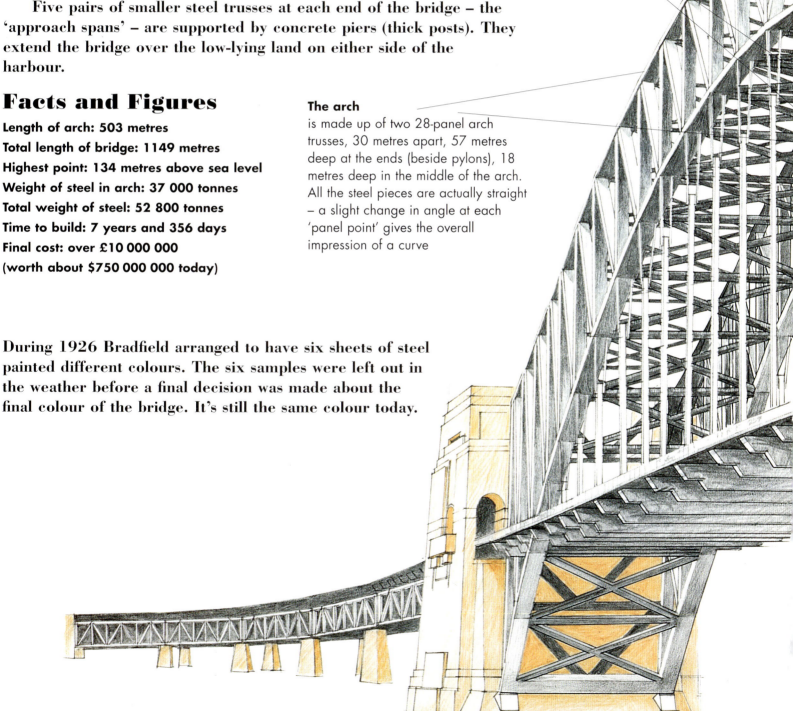

Panel points

Hangers, one suspended from each lower panel point

The arch
is made up of two 28-panel arch trusses, 30 metres apart, 57 metres deep at the ends (beside pylons), 18 metres deep in the middle of the arch. All the steel pieces are actually straight – a slight change in angle at each 'panel point' gives the overall impression of a curve

First Things First

Dorman, Long and Co.'s first job was to level a large area of land by the harbour at North Sydney – the area now occupied by Luna Park and the North Sydney Pool. They excavated 34 000 cubic metres of rock from the cliffs and pushed it into the sea, creating flat land large enough for two huge workshops. They also built wharves where ships could unload bulk steel from England and Newcastle (Australia), and from which barges could carry the finished pieces of steelwork out to the bridge.

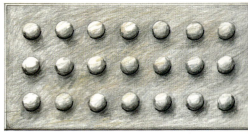

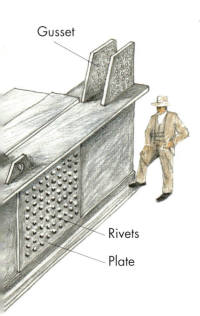

Gusset

Rivets

Plate

▶ **Plan of proposed bridge and workshops**
The 'Heavy Workshop' (150 metres long x 46 metres wide) was where workers cut large pieces of steel to the right size and shape, drilled all the necessary holes in them and then joined them together to make the main parts of the bridge. For example, the bottom chords of the arch (see diagram left) are divided into 28 lengths, each about 20 metres long, up to 2.5 metres deep and over 3 metres wide. Each was made up in the Heavy Workshop out of four webs (up and down bits) and two flanges (top and bottom), all joined together with steel plates, angles and rivets, and further strengthened in places with extra plates riveted on. Still more steel plates called 'gussets' were added, ready to join on to the neighbouring parts of the bridge. Neighbouring parts that had to be bolted and riveted together on the bridge (away from the workshop) were fixed together first in the workshop, to make sure they fitted.
The downstairs section of the 'Light Workshop' (180 metres x 40 metres) was where workers assembled the smaller parts of the bridge. Upstairs, carpenters made full-size templates (patterns) out of timber for nearly all the steelwork.

During 1925 Dorman, Long started demolishing all the buildings that were going to be in the way. Most of these were houses – 438 altogether – mainly rented by waterside workers and their families. Building owners were compensated for the loss of their buildings, but the people who lived there were not. Nor were they helped to find other accommodation. Most had difficulty finding anywhere else to live, often ending up far away from their work and friends.

---

26 March 1925
In one of the many ceremonies held at different times to mark the beginning of work on the Sydney Harbour Bridge, the New South Wales Minister for Public Works lays the foundation stone of the southern abutment (see pp 14–15).

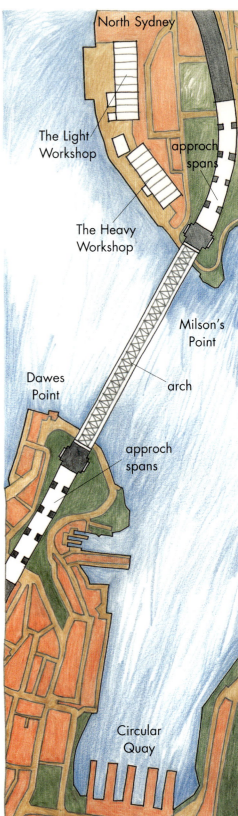

North Sydney

The Light Workshop

approch spans

The Heavy Workshop

Dawes Point

Milson's Point

arch

approch spans

Circular Quay

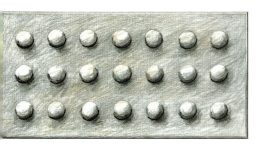

Approach Spans

Work on the Sydney Harbour Bridge began at both ends at the same time, and moved gradually inwards, to meet in the middle about five years later.

While the Light and Heavy workshops were being built at North Sydney, work had already begun on the approach spans – five at each end of the bridge – all supported on pairs of concrete piers.

January 1925

Excavations begin for the concrete footings (foundations) on which the piers and the abutments at either end of the bridge will be built. The abutments, the pylons on top of the abutments and all of the piers will be built of concrete and faced with stone. The stone will not help to carry the weight of the bridge – it's just there to look good. The stone chosen for the job is granite, a very hard, strong material. It will be quarried at Moruya, a coastal town about 300 km south of Sydney.

7 October 1925

The first block of stone is laid. Altogether around 40 000 blocks of stone will have to be cut at Moruya. Each block must be cut to exactly the right size and shape according to detailed engineers' drawings, and then marked with a number, so that the workers on the bridge will know where to put it.

September 1926

The concrete piers to support the approach spans are finished.

Steel 'ties' built into the concrete corresponded with the bed joints (horizontal mortar joints) of the blockwork

Some blocks had the corners neatly chiseled, but the faces were left rough

▲ **Concrete pier with stone facings**

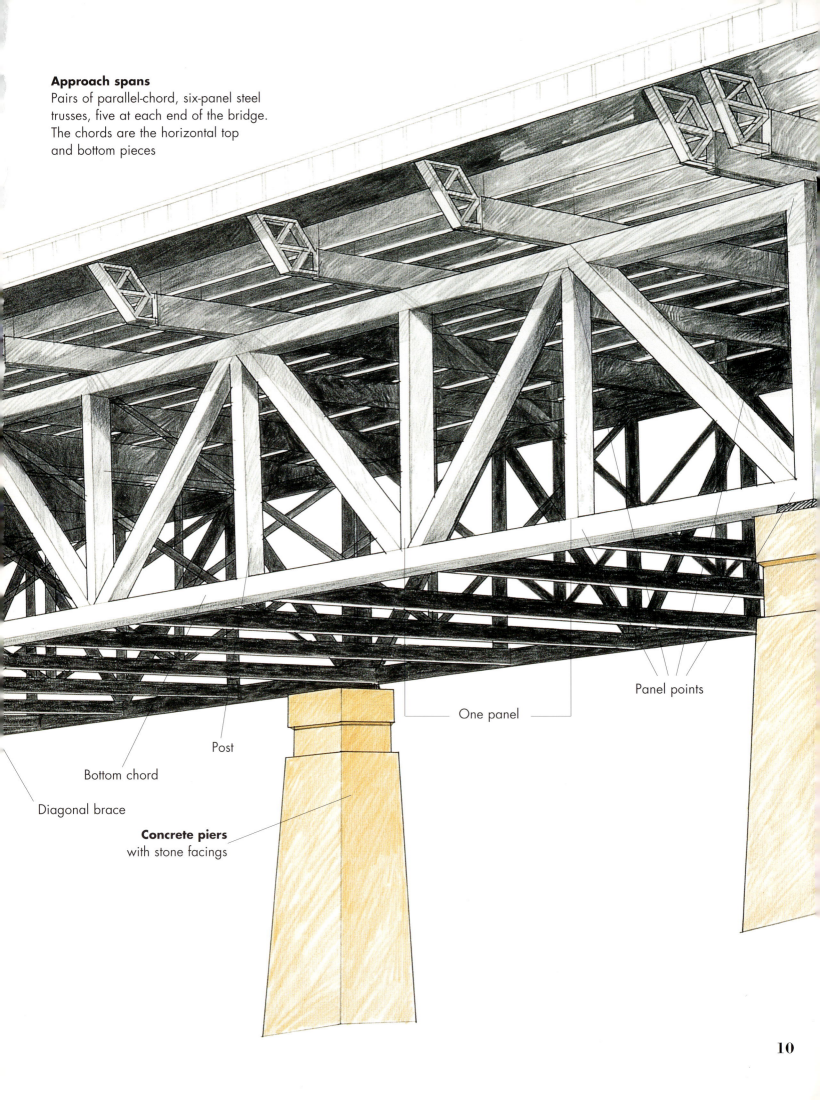

Approach spans
Pairs of parallel-chord, six-panel steel trusses, five at each end of the bridge. The chords are the horizontal top and bottom pieces

Panel points

One panel

Post

Bottom chord

Diagonal brace

Concrete piers
with stone facings

Concrete pylons
with stone facings, sitting
on top of the abutments.
Total height, 87 metres

Top chord

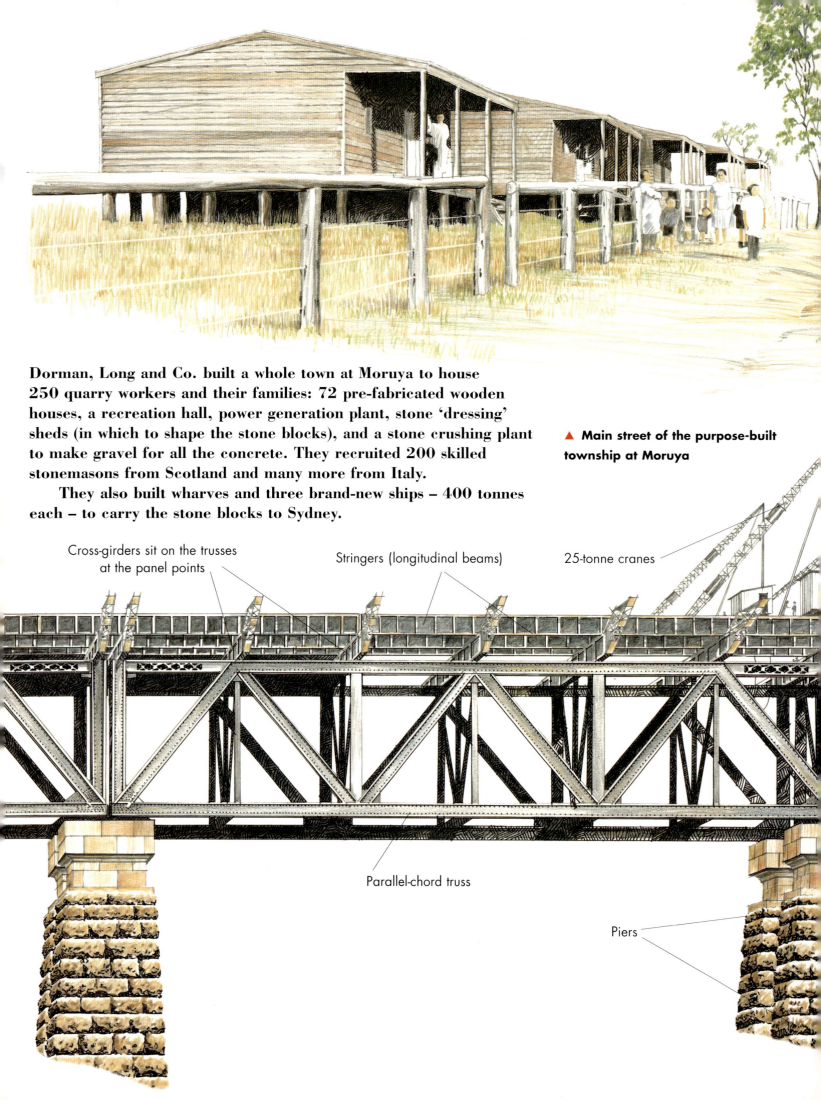

Dorman, Long and Co. built a whole town at Moruya to house 250 quarry workers and their families: 72 pre-fabricated wooden houses, a recreation hall, power generation plant, stone 'dressing' sheds (in which to shape the stone blocks), and a stone crushing plant to make gravel for all the concrete. They recruited 200 skilled stonemasons from Scotland and many more from Italy.

They also built wharves and three brand-new ships – 400 tonnes each – to carry the stone blocks to Sydney.

▲ **Main street of the purpose-built township at Moruya**

Cross-girders sit on the trusses at the panel points

Stringers (longitudinal beams)

25-tonne cranes

Parallel-chord truss

Piers

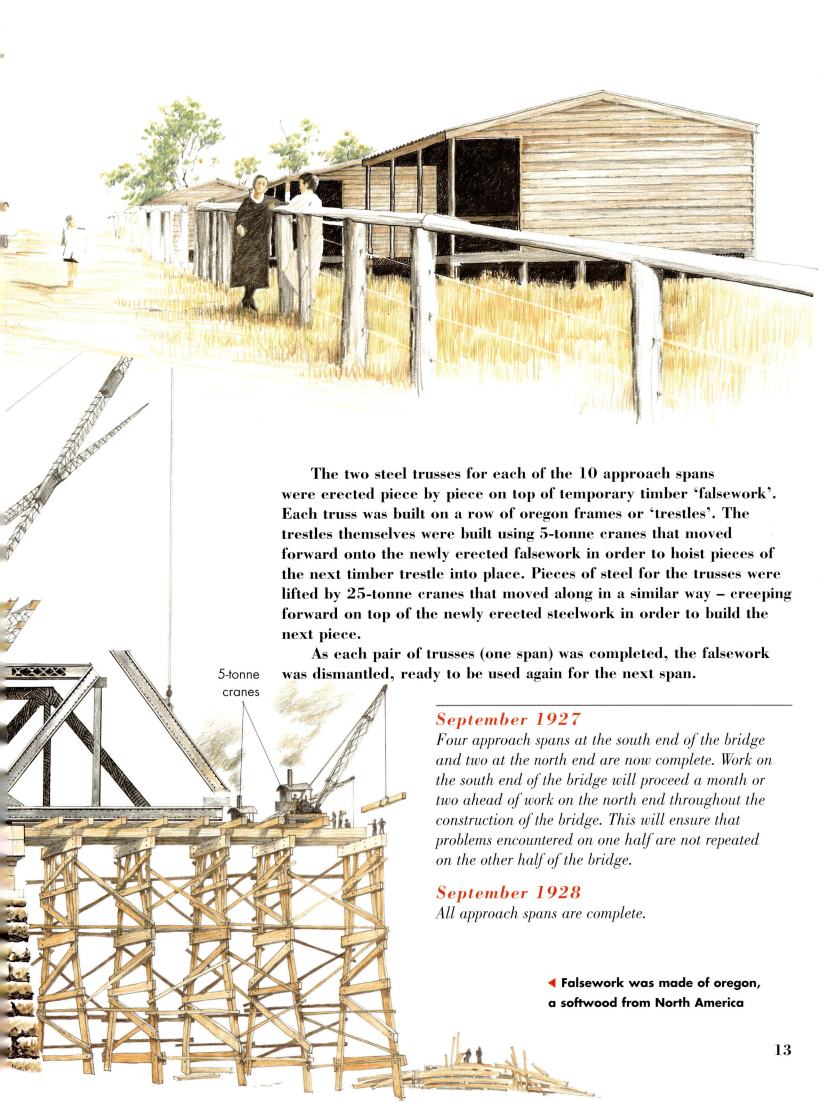

The two steel trusses for each of the 10 approach spans were erected piece by piece on top of temporary timber 'falsework'. Each truss was built on a row of oregon frames or 'trestles'. The trestles themselves were built using 5-tonne cranes that moved forward onto the newly erected falsework in order to hoist pieces of the next timber trestle into place. Pieces of steel for the trusses were lifted by 25-tonne cranes that moved along in a similar way – creeping forward on top of the newly erected steelwork in order to build the next piece.

As each pair of trusses (one span) was completed, the falsework was dismantled, ready to be used again for the next span.

5-tonne cranes

September 1927

Four approach spans at the south end of the bridge and two at the north end are now complete. Work on the south end of the bridge will proceed a month or two ahead of work on the north end throughout the construction of the bridge. This will ensure that problems encountered on one half are not repeated on the other half of the bridge.

September 1928

All approach spans are complete.

◀ Falsework was made of oregon, a softwood from North America

13

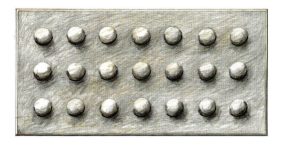

Abutments

The final approach spans brought the bridge-builders at last to the abutments – those massive stone-faced concrete structures at either end of the main arch. The concrete footings for the abutments, and for the tall pylons that sit on top of them, also serve as 'skewbacks', or angled foundations. These hold the whole weight of the steel arch and prevent it from spreading outwards – a bit like someone's foot holding the bottom of a ladder. To make the footings, the builders excavated huge holes in the solid sandstone on either side of the harbour and filled them with concrete. The concrete was poured in specially designed hexagonal batches because the engineers thought this would transfer the huge weight of the bridge most evenly onto the sandstone beneath.

Once the abutments were finished to bridge-deck level, the 25-tonne cranes were used to build a steel ramp on each of them and assemble the huge 'creeper cranes' on the ramps. The creeper cranes would later creep off the ramps onto the steel arch itself and then move gradually up and out, building the steelwork in front of them as they went.

There was one creeper crane on each side of the harbour.

▼ **Abutment footings or skewbacks: 27 metres wide x 12 metres front to back x 9 metres deep**

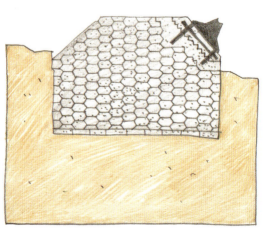

14

The creeper cranes were each in fact five cranes on one travelling base:
- the **main crane**, which could also travel from side to side (to work on both trusses), had a lifting capacity of 124 tonnes;
- **two smaller cranes at the back** of the platform, used to lift small loads;
- another **two smaller 'jigger' cranes at the front**, mainly to control the position and angle of the load being lifted.

The whole thing weighed 610 tonnes. The operator communicated by telephone with the riggers who were bolting each new piece of steel into place.

Temporary struts placed between the end posts and the abutments

Bearing

Christmas 1928

Sitting on the southern ramp, the creeper crane is now ready to hoist some of the largest and heaviest steel assemblies to begin the arch. These are:
- *the cast steel bearings and pins that transfer the whole weight of the bridge to the skewbacks;*
- *the first panel of each arch, comprising bottom and top chords, two posts and one diagonal brace;*
- *lateral bracing between the two arches.*

March 1929

The first panel has been completely assembled and braced. Now the creeper crane can edge off the ramp at last and onto the bridge, to begin its laborious progress up the slope. Its first job: assembling the second panel.

The Next Step

Almost from the start, the engineers had grappled with two major problems calling for audacious solutions.
- First, they had to work out how to keep both sides of the unfinished arch up in the air as they were gradually extended, further and further out over the harbour. Once completed, of course, the two sides of the arch would keep each other up by leaning against each other, but in the meantime thousands of tonnes of steel had to be stopped from crashing down into the water. Falsework had been used to hold up the approach spans, but that was clearly not possible here. The engineers' ingenious solution to this problem is shown on pages 18-19.
- The second question was what to do about changes in temperature . . .

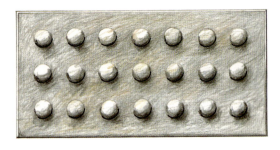

The Hinges

One of the problems with building things out of steel is that it expands as it warms up (on a hot day, for example), and contracts as it cools down. With flat bridges it's easy to deal with this problem. The builders fix one end of the bridge to one abutment, but sit the other end on rollers, allowing it to slide backwards and forwards on the rollers as it gets longer and shorter.

The Sydney Harbour Bridge, however, is held in at both ends by the abutments – it has to be, otherwise the arch would simply flatten out and collapse. So when it gets hot, there's only one place for it to go – up. The top of the arch actually rises and falls about 180 mm due to changes in the temperature! To allow for this, Freeman and his team designed 'hinges', shown in the diagram.

▼ **Flat steel bridge**

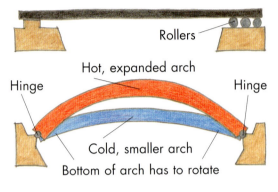

Rollers

Hot, expanded arch

Hinge   Hinge

Cold, smaller arch

Bottom of arch has to rotate

▲ **Steel-arch bridge**

▼ There are four 'hinges' altogether, two at each end, and they are truly massive! Each one is cradled in a huge cast steel 'saddle', which transfers the load to the concrete skewback

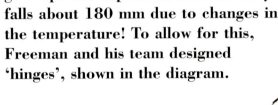

Pin (hinge)
A cast steel rod 4.2 metres long, 368 mm in diameter. It sits in a curved saddle exactly the right diameter to hold it. Another saddle, upside-down and fixed to the bottom of the bridge, sits on top of the pin

Two 24-mm thick steel 'webs' and 10 steel 'diaphragms' carry the load to the steel base, 7.2 metres x 6.3 metres

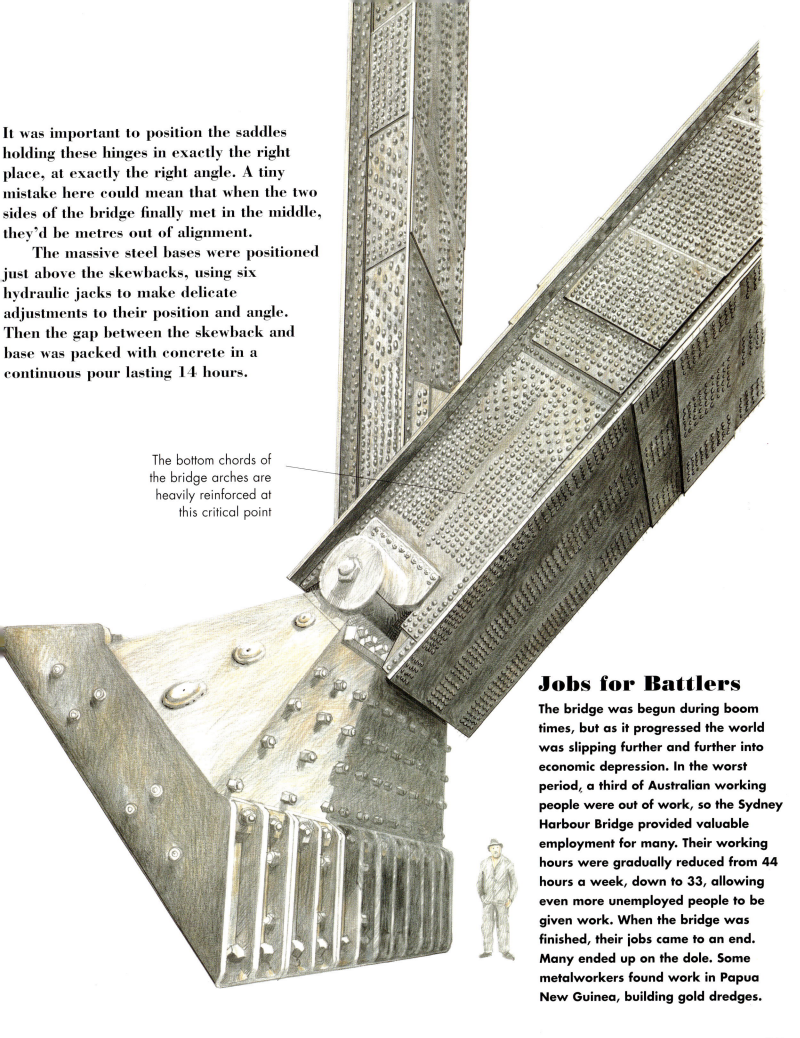

It was important to position the saddles holding these hinges in exactly the right place, at exactly the right angle. A tiny mistake here could mean that when the two sides of the bridge finally met in the middle, they'd be metres out of alignment.

The massive steel bases were positioned just above the skewbacks, using six hydraulic jacks to make delicate adjustments to their position and angle. Then the gap between the skewback and base was packed with concrete in a continuous pour lasting 14 hours.

The bottom chords of the bridge arches are heavily reinforced at this critical point

Jobs for Battlers

The bridge was begun during boom times, but as it progressed the world was slipping further and further into economic depression. In the worst period, a third of Australian working people were out of work, so the Sydney Harbour Bridge provided valuable employment for many. Their working hours were gradually reduced from 44 hours a week, down to 33, allowing even more unemployed people to be given work. When the bridge was finished, their jobs came to an end. Many ended up on the dole. Some metalworkers found work in Papua New Guinea, building gold dredges.

Holding Up the Unfinished Arch

None of Sydney's famous sandstone was used in the bridge – not even for the stone facings on the abutments – but without it the Sydney Harbour Bridge could never have been built.

The city of Sydney and many of its suburbs – on both sides of the harbour – are built on a solid reef of sandstone bedrock. Sandstone is easily cut and tunnelled, allowing Sydney's underground rail network to be built at around the same time as the bridge (also under the direction of J.J.C. Bradfield). Perhaps that gave him the idea of cutting out two huge horseshoe-shaped tunnels, one on each side of the harbour, threading hundreds of thick steel cables through them, and fixing the cables to the ends of the unfinished bridge. These cables held back the weight of each unfinished half-arch, stopping it from rotating on those massive pins and flopping down into the harbour. As more and more steel was added to the bridge, more and more cables were added to hold the weight.

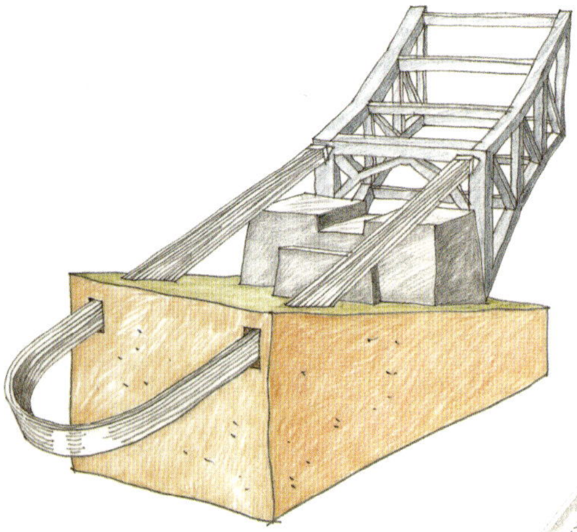

▶ One hundred and twenty-eight cables were fixed to each end of the bridge and threaded through horseshoe-shaped tunnels in the sandstone. Each cable, 365 metres long, 70 mm in diameter and 8.6 tonnes in weight, was made up of 217 individual wires. The cables were each designed to withstand a load of 467 tonnes, but in fact they were never called upon to take more than 117 tonnes

▲ The cables were fixed to these massive steel brackets

Light Workshop

Heavy Workshop

Laurence Ennis established Dorman, Long and Co.'s site office in this building near Dawe's Point

26 October 1928

The 40-metre long cable tunnels are now complete and the first cables can be run through them, fixed to special butterfly-shaped attachments on the end posts of the bridge, and tensioned. Hydraulic jacks will be used to tension the cables. Each will be checked regularly to make sure it is taking an equal share of the load.

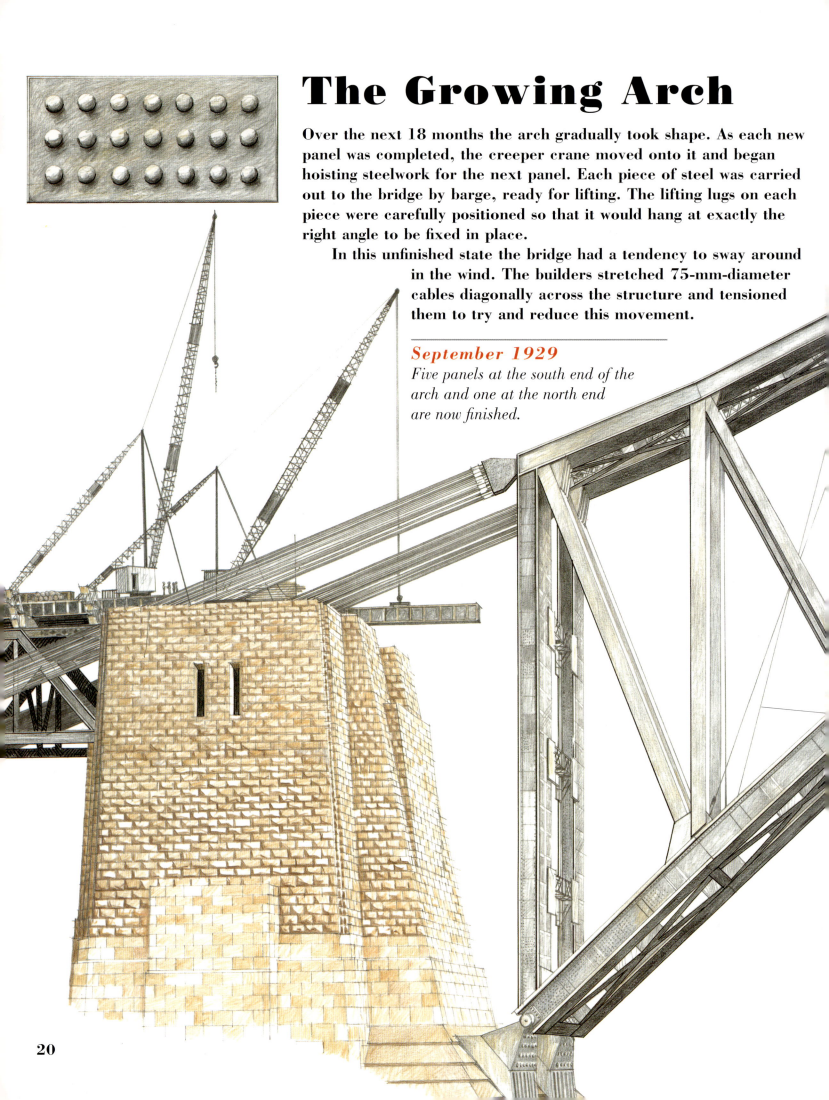

The Growing Arch

Over the next 18 months the arch gradually took shape. As each new panel was completed, the creeper crane moved onto it and began hoisting steelwork for the next panel. Each piece of steel was carried out to the bridge by barge, ready for lifting. The lifting lugs on each piece were carefully positioned so that it would hang at exactly the right angle to be fixed in place.

In this unfinished state the bridge had a tendency to sway around in the wind. The builders stretched 75-mm-diameter cables diagonally across the structure and tensioned them to try and reduce this movement.

September 1929

Five panels at the south end of the arch and one at the north end are now finished.

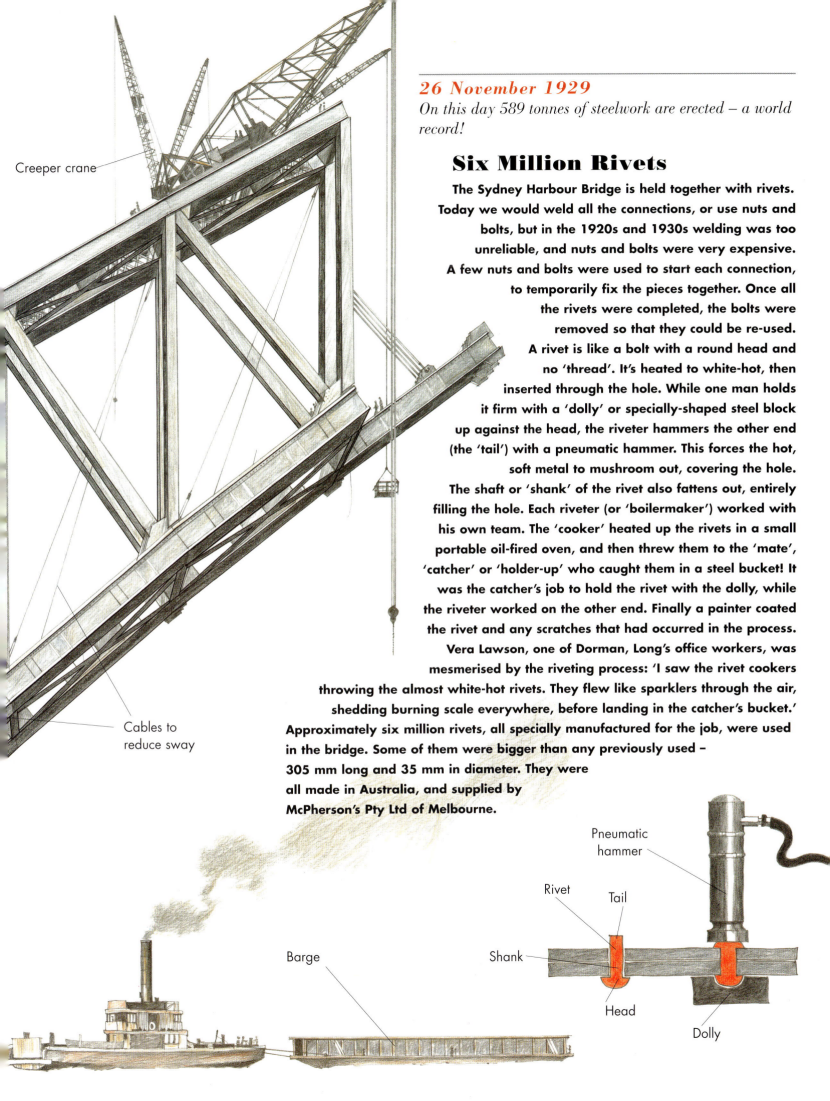

Creeper crane

Cables to
reduce sway

Six Million Rivets

The Sydney Harbour Bridge is held together with rivets. Today we would weld all the connections, or use nuts and bolts, but in the 1920s and 1930s welding was too unreliable, and nuts and bolts were very expensive. A few nuts and bolts were used to start each connection, to temporarily fix the pieces together. Once all the rivets were completed, the bolts were removed so that they could be re-used.

A rivet is like a bolt with a round head and no 'thread'. It's heated to white-hot, then inserted through the hole. While one man holds it firm with a 'dolly' or specially-shaped steel block up against the head, the riveter hammers the other end (the 'tail') with a pneumatic hammer. This forces the hot, soft metal to mushroom out, covering the hole. The shaft or 'shank' of the rivet also fattens out, entirely filling the hole. Each riveter (or 'boilermaker') worked with his own team. The 'cooker' heated up the rivets in a small portable oil-fired oven, and then threw them to the 'mate', 'catcher' or 'holder-up' who caught them in a steel bucket! It was the catcher's job to hold the rivet with the dolly, while the riveter worked on the other end. Finally a painter coated the rivet and any scratches that had occurred in the process.

Vera Lawson, one of Dorman, Long's office workers, was mesmerised by the riveting process: 'I saw the rivet cookers throwing the almost white-hot rivets. They flew like sparklers through the air, shedding burning scale everywhere, before landing in the catcher's bucket.'

Approximately six million rivets, all specially manufactured for the job, were used in the bridge. Some of them were bigger than any previously used – 305 mm long and 35 mm in diameter. They were all made in Australia, and supplied by McPherson's Pty Ltd of Melbourne.

Pneumatic hammer

Rivet

Tail

Shank

Head

Dolly

Barge

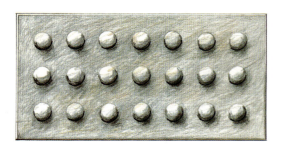

Working on the Bridge

'There was nowhere to stand,' said Harry Tomrop, one of the most experienced steel erectors working on the bridge. 'We were hanging on by our eyelashes.'

He was talking about the difficulties encountered erecting the jib or 'arm' of the creeper crane, before work on the arch had even started. Soon George Scott was finding it 'hard to keep from falling down the steep part of the arch'. At one stage Scott got a smack in the mouth from a red-hot rivet flying through the air. He had to pay for a new set of false teeth out of his own pocket!

There were no safety rails or nets, little or no scaffolding and no helmets – all basic safety features that we now take for granted. There were no earmuffs, either, and most of the ironworkers and boiler-makers later suffered hearing problems. Dorman, Long and Co. and the New South Wales government seem to have had a callous disregard for workers' safety.

But the men seemed, if anything, proud to work without these 'soft luxuries', proud of their ability to monkey around on delicate steel webs, suspended at such dizzying heights above the harbour. And the safety record for the project, under the circumstances, was not too bad. Altogether there were 16 workers killed – only seven on the bridge itself. Fifty-six people died building the Forth Bridge in England and 139 on the Brooklyn Bridge in the USA, both in the 1880s; 121 people died working on the Snowy Mountains Scheme in Australia in the 1950s and 1960s.

Dogmen and Tin Hares

For eight years, between 1200 and 1400 men were working on the bridge, in the workshops or at Moruya at any one time. Most of the steelwork was put together by about 150 riggers. They came from all over the world: Scotland, Ireland, England, Scandinavia, Canada, the USA, Malta. The riveting in the workshops and on the bridge was done by boilermakers, aided by mates, cookers and painters (see p. 21). Dogmen helped co-ordinate the hoisting of loads, sometimes riding the steel up from the barges, and communicating by telephone with the crane-drivers. And there were dozens of other occupations: stonemasons, concretors, ironworkers, carpenters, asphalters, electricians, plumbers, seamen and labourers.

Amazingly, there were only 12 officially appointed 'steel erectors', six on each side of the bridge. This select band, dubbed the 'tin hares', were the ones who jockeyed each steel piece into position, and fastened the first nuts and bolts to hold it in place, finely adjusting the angle and position before riveting began.

Of course, many more people worked for other companies (apart from Dorman, Long and Co.), manu-facturing or supplying paint, rivets, wire, pipes, timber, cement, equipment, oil and the thousands of other items needed for such a huge job.

Death on the Bridge

The same two perils are always lurking around big constructions sites: things dropping on you, and falling off things.

Felix Faulkner, for example, one of the 'tin hares', was hit by a half-tonne steel plate in 1931. He died a few hours later.

Jack Rue, a young boy doing odd jobs around the workshops, told a story about an ironworker who was 'bolting up stitch plates for the riveters. His long-handled spanner slipped and he went over backwards. A diver found his body later, standing upright in the mud'.

When the platform that Thomas McKeon and two others were standing on started to fall, his companions grabbed at the bridge structure and held on for dear life. But as McKeon fell he lunged desperately for some chains hanging from a crane, only to become entangled in them. So fast was he going that the chains ripped off a leg and a hand before he hit the ground.

The last death on the bridge was also a fall. James Campbell, a foreman rigger, was dismantling the scaffolding used to clean down stonework on the pylons when a gust of wind caught the pole supporting him and he fell. Witnesses described him turning over and over in the air as he plummeted nearly 50 metres before his head was severed by a steel bracket holding a street light.

Others had miraculous escapes. Jack Rue said: 'A bloke called Kelly fell 150 feet [nearly 50 metres] off the deck of the bridge into the water and survived with two broken ribs. When they got him out his boots were split right open and were up around his thighs. They gave him a gold watch'.

Others lost limbs and fingers, but lived. As Laurence Ennis put it, 'Every day those men went on to the bridge, they went...not knowing whether they would come down alive or not.'

The Arch Meets

During 1930, Sydneysiders were able to watch the progress of the arch as they went about their daily lives. Gradually the two sides edged closed and closer together.

4 August 1930

The northern half-arch is complete, having caught up with and edged ahead of work on the south side.

7 August 1930

The southern half-arch is finished, leaving a gap between the two sides of about 1 metre. A short plank is laid across the gap and the supervising engineer, Laurence Ennis, is first to 'cross' the Sydney Harbour Bridge. He gives the order to start lengthening the tie-back cables, to allow the two halves to tilt slowly toward each other.

Workers took nearly eight days to lengthen all the cables sufficiently, by loosening nuts and long threaded rods attaching each end of each cable to the bridge. They eased every nut – 512 in all – by just a few turns at a time, before starting the whole process again... and again... and again.

13 August 1930

A violent windstorm hits Sydney, buffeting the two sides of the arch – now in their most vulnerable state – causing them to sway from side to side, often in opposite directions to each other. The engineers hold their breaths, but the bridge stands up to the test.

Rivet heater

When the two sides of the arch were finished, they lined up almost perfectly – a credit to the accuracy of every stage of the work. To get them to meet exactly, a massive tapered guiding pin was mounted on each bottom chord of one half-arch, with a square hole to accept each pin on the other. Once the two sides were finally leaning in against each other, a large horizontal round pin on one side, and corresponding semi-circular groove in the other acted like a hinge, similar to those at the base of the arch (see pp. 16-17).

Guiding pin

Hinge pin

*11 a.m. The gap is down to 114 mm on the east side and
120 mm on the west.*

*4.15 p.m. The two sides finally touch, but shortly afterwards they separate as
the day cools and the bridge steel contracts.*

*10 p.m. After more work on the cables, the two sides have touched again, this
time for good.*

There were only five men on the top of the arch when the
two sides of the bridge finally came together. Standing there
in the dark to witness this dramatic moment,
Laurence Ennis later recalled, 'We were so
overawed with the mightiness of it all
that we did not speak'.

Diagonal brace

Bottom chord

Lateral brace

9 September 1930

*The last posts and pieces of top chord are now in place
and the arch can be completed.*

With just the bottom chords meeting, almost all the load was being
carried by that part of the arch truss. To allow the top chord to take
its share of the load, workers placed large pneumatic jacks in the gaps
left in the top chord. The jacks, applying a pressure of 8400 tonnes,
forced the two halves of the bridge apart, taking some of the load off
the bottom chord and making the top chord do its share of the work.
The gaps were then filled with permanent steel packers, and the
jacks were removed. During this process the top of the bridge
rose 320 mm, because the bottom chord lengthened as the huge
pressure on it was relieved.

Only now were the top and bottom chord connections riveted to
form rigid joints.

Over the course of the following week, the cables were slackened
off until they ceased to carry any share of the load at all. The two sides
of the arch were now supported entirely by leaning against each other.

Lots of Arithmetic

Ralph Freeman and his team of
engineers had to calculate the size
of each piece of steel in the bridge,
not just once, but three times. They had
to ensure the structure would hold up:

1 when it was held back by the cables,
   and the steelwork was 'cantilevered'
   (sticking out) over the harbour;

2 for that short period when only the
   bottom chords were leaning against
   each other;

3 when both top and bottom chords
   were rigidly joined, and the load of
   the deck and traffic was added.

Hangers and Deck

Dorman, Long and Co. lost no time in finishing the job, apart from giving all workers a half-day off to celebrate the joining of the arch. The creeper cranes now retreated back down the slope. But as they went they still had work to do – lifting the long hangers that suspend the bridge deck from the arch, and the heavy steel framework of the deck itself. This part of the job took just nine months.

Access panels for riveter's mates, painters and others who had to work inside the box chords

Men working in the dark inside the huge box chords and girders were showered with red-hot scales of metal from rivets being hammered into place above them, and constantly cut themselves on metal shavings lying around. A pair of overalls could be cut to ribbons in a couple of weeks

Hangers

The hangers were hoisted into place using the main crane to take the weight, and a jigger crane to rotate it from horizontal to vertical.

A special cradle was needed to lift the hangers, because they had to be hoisted to a position directly *under* the arch truss. Now that the arch was finished, the crane could only lift things up *beside* the trusses.

As each new hanger was hoisted, a rigger rode up on its top, so he could make the first bolted connections to the underside of the bottom chord.

The longest hanger was 58.8 metres long, the shortest 7.3 metres.

---

23 September 1930
The first and largest hanger is ferried out from the workshop, but before it is lifted a wild storm blows up and the barge is speedily towed back.

Pin

Cross-girders

Each pair of hangers supported a cross-girder. At 48.7 metres long and weighing 110 tonnes, the cross-girders were the heaviest pieces of the bridge to be lifted.

Each cross-girder was connected to the hangers with just two pins – one for each hanger. These huge pins were banged through the holes by four men using large wooden battering rams!

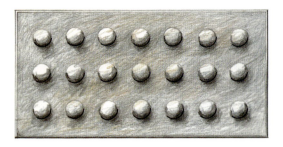

Testing the Bridge

There can have been little doubt in anyone's mind about the strength of the Sydney Harbour Bridge and its ability to do the job for which it was designed. But the conscientious and meticulous J.J.C. Bradfield had still arranged a series of punishing tests for the structure. Ninety-six railway engines weighing a total of 7.6 tonnes were shunted onto the bridge in various arrangements. First one side was loaded up and then the other; next one end, then the other; loads were concentrated on the critical 'quarter points' of the span; and many other arrangements were tried. Freeman and Ennis later complained that Bradfield had actually overloaded the bridge by 20 per cent during this process. Thousands of measurements were taken over a three-week period to check the deflection or deformation of the bridge under these severe strains. The results, apparently, were satisfactory.

▶ The 1932 equivalent of today's cricket-match streaker: ex-captain de Groote is bundled off to the local police lock-up, after cutting the ribbon at the opening ceremony.

Finishing Touches

Once the tie-back cables were released, work on the pylons could go ahead. The cables had stretched over the abutments, preventing this. They were finished by the end of 1931. One of them now houses a museum.

During 1931 all manner of other finishing work went ahead: concreting the bridge deck and then laying asphalt on the concrete, installing all the power and telephone lines and the water, gas and drainage pipes that the bridge would also carry over the harbour, carrying out new roadworks and changes to existing roads at either end of the bridge, laying the railway and tram tracks across it, and generally cleaning up.

---

12 January 1932
Dorman, Long and Co. makes the bridge available to the New South Wales government for testing.

15 March 1932
Dorman, Long and Co. formally hands over the bridge to the government of New South Wales.

16 March 1932
Childrens' Day – a Wednesday – sees some 10 000 schoolchildren walking across the bridge in the pouring rain, three days before anyone else will be allowed to. Unfortunately, it rains all day.

The Opening

The opening of the Sydney Harbour Bridge in 1932 was a huge event – a bit like an Olympic Games or the Year 2000 celebrations. The opening ceremony itself was just one of the many events planned to celebrate the completion of the bridge. In addition there were boat races, an Air Force flying demonstration, fireworks, art exhibitions, balls and dinners, speedboat manoeuvres, a race meeting, a tennis tournament, a cricket match and a parade of boats and ships. The whole party lasted about two weeks.

---

19 March 1932

A beautiful sunny day for the official opening. Some people think that the King or another member of the Royal family should have been invited to open the bridge, but Premier Jack Lang has decided to do the job himself.

▲ Children from Fort Street School – the last stage of a 550-km relay – bring a message of congratulations from kids in the outback

The ceremonies started with a message of congratulations from the King, followed by speeches from the Governor (Sir Philip Game), the Minister for Public Works, a director of Dorman, Long and Co., and finally Laurence Ennis. As the ceremony approached its climax, two children from the nearby Fort Street Boys' and Girls' School arrived bringing a message that had been carried by relays of school children, running all the way from Tottenham, 550 kilometres away in north-western New South Wales.

But before Premier Lang could cut the ribbon and declare the bridge finally open, there was to be one more dramatic event. A lone horseman in a military uniform galloped up and slashed the ribbon with his sword, declaring the bridge open 'in the name of the decent and loyal citizens of New South Wales'. He was ex-captain F.E de Groote, a member of the 'New Guard' – an extreme para-military organisation. Its members had been enraged when royalty was not invited to open the bridge. De Groote was dragged from his horse and bundled off to the local police station. The ribbon was hastily re-tied and Lang performed the official opening ceremony, accompanied by a 21-gun salute and an Air Force fly-past.

A similar ceremony was conducted at the other end of the bridge by Alderman Primrose, the mayor of North Sydney. Coincidentally, Primrose was also a member of the New Guard!

Finally a 2-km-long parade wound its way over the bridge. It was led by the band of the 'Youth Australia League', closely followed by 328 school children. Then came 100 Harbour Bridge workers, 20 Aborigines, and dozens of other representative groups, commercial floats and marching bands.

The Bridge Today

In 1988 the New South Wales government finally repaid the last money borrowed to finance the project – 18 months after beginning work on a tunnel to carry traffic under the harbour.

The final cost of the bridge was £10 057 170 pounds, 7 shillings and 9 pence.

As well as its pivotal role in Sydney's transport systems, the 'giant coat-hanger' serves as a spectacular platform for fireworks displays, a challenging walk for those who are rich, fit and brave enough to join one of the guided tours of the arch, and even a useful place for army and emergency services people to practise their abseiling skills.

In 1932, the year it opened, 11 000 vehicles used the bridge. The list of tolls for that year is a useful reminder of just how much things have changed in 70 years:

Motor cars and motorcycles with side cars	6 pence
Sulkies, buggies and hand carts	3 pence
Vans, lorries, drays, wagons over 2 tons	1 shilling
Horse and rider	3 pence
Horses and cattle as loose stock	2 pence/head
Sheep or pigs	1 penny/head

The Sydney Harbour Bridge remains Australia's most identifiable symbol. No one who stands close to the massive bearing pins or looks up at the maze of steel that makes up the arches can fail to marvel at its enormous scale and organic, dinosaurean shape, or to glory in the sheer inventiveness and audacity of its designers and builders.

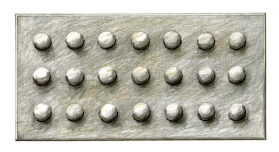

Glossary

abutment a structure that supports the end of a bridge

angle piece of steel with right-angle-shaped cross-section

asphalt flexible road-surfacing material made of a mixture of gravel and bitumen (heavy thick oil)

barge long, flat-bottomed boat for carrying freight on rivers and harbours

brace piece of steel or timber, usually used diagonally to stiffen a right-angle joint between two other pieces

causeway a raised road across wet ground or water

chords top and bottom pieces, usually horizontal, of a truss

contract a legally binding agreement, usually written, between two people.

creeper crane travelling or moving crane

deck (of a bridge) flat part of a bridge holding the road or railway

depression a long period of decline in business, financial and industrial activity resulting in widespread unemployment

dole money paid by a government to unemployed people

engineer person who designs structures, using mathematics to calculate the size of structural pieces

excavation digging holes in the ground to reach underground rock or ground hard enough to build on

facing attractive covering, often in stone or brickwork, on the load-carrying bits of a building or structure

falsework temporary, usually timber, framework built to support bits of the permanent structure until they are properly attached and self-supporting

flanges the horizontal top and bottom pieces of a steel I-beam or box-beam

footings the lowest part of a building or structure, usually concrete, which transfers the weight of the structure to the ground: sometimes called foundations

foundations the base that a structure rests on (see also footings)

foundation stone ceremonial stone laid or placed in position to mark the beginning of construction of a major building or structure

girder large steel beam made up of lots of smaller pieces of steel

gusset steel plate used to connect two pieces of steel together

hanger vertical steel piece, hanging from the arch, supporting the bridge deck

jigger crane small crane used to assist in the positioning of heavy loads supported by a large crane

lifting lug a projection with a hole in it, fixed to a large object so it can be lifted by a crane

panel (of a truss) section of truss between two posts (one post and the next)

pier pillar or post carrying a load down to the ground.

plate flat piece of steel

pneumatic using compressed air to transfer power from one place to another – e.g. pneumatic jack, pneumatic drill

pylon one of a pair of towers or high structures marking an entrance

quarter points the points one quarter of the way across a span from each end – the points at which the bridge is under most stress

rigger person who erects steel structures, specialising in working on very high structures

riveting method of fixing two or more metal plates together using a metal pin with a flange or head on one end. The pin is pushed through a hole and the other end is spread out to form another head

scaffolding temporary platform for workers to stand on

shank the long straight piece of a rivet, bolt or screw

skewback footing with an angled top surface carrying the load of an arched bridge to solid ground

span each unsupported part of a bridge, from one support to another

stonemason person who cuts, prepares and builds with stone

stringer longitudinal (lengthways) structural member in a structural framework

strut a structural piece that is 'in compression' (i.e. the load is pushing in on the ends, rather than pulling on the ends)

template a pattern, usually made of thin timber, used as a guide for cutting steel to the right shape and drilling holes in the right places

tender an offer in writing to do certain work in return for a certain amount of money

trestle temporary or permanent timber frame supporting a bridge

truss frame made of lots of 'sticks' of timber or steel, fixed together to form lots of triangles. Trusses are used to span bigger distances and/or to carry greater loads than a simple beam would manage

webs the vertical (up-and-down) pieces of a steel I-beam or box-beam

Index